Motocross™

Supercross

Janey Levy

PowerKiDS
press
New York

To Tyrone, for his patience and for teaching me about motor sports

Published in 2007 by The Rosen Publishing Group, Inc.
29 East 21st Street, New York, NY 10010

First Edition

Editor: Joanne Randolph
Book Design: Ginny Chu
Layout Design: Kate Laczynski

Photo Credits: Cover, pp. 1, 4–5, 8–15, 17–24 © Simon Cudby Photo; p. 7 © Luis Gene/AFP/Getty Images; pp. 26–27 © Robert Cianflone/All Sport/Getty Images; p. 29 © Cristina Quicler/AFP/Getty Images.

Library of Congress Cataloging-in-Publication Data

Levy, Janey.
   Supercross / Janey Levy. — 1st ed.
        p. cm. — (Motocross)
   Includes index.
   ISBN-13: 978-1-4042-3693-6 (library binding)
   ISBN-10: 1-4042-3693-7 (library binding)
   1. Supercross—Juvenile literature. I. Title.
   GV1060.1455.L48 2007
   796.7'56—dc22
                                                    2006030321

Manufactured in the United States of America

Contents

Supercross (SX) is a special form of motocross (MX). Both are motorcycle races on dirt tracks with twists, turns, hills, and jumps. Motocross takes place in a country area on a track that has lots of natural features. Supercross takes place in a sports stadium on a dirt track that is man-made and built just for the race.

These riders are racing in the Dallas Supercross event in 2006.

Motocross, which was originally known as scrambling, began in the United States in 1959. It was slow to become popular, though. Then, in 1971, a motocross race was held on

Ricky Carmichael rode to victory in the 2006 Supercross race in Atlanta, Georgia.

a man-made track at Daytona International Speedway, in Florida. The speedway is a famous racetrack used for hugely popular NASCAR racing.

The following year a motocross race was held on a man-made track at Los Angeles Memorial Coliseum. The coliseum is a stadium used for football, soccer, and special events. The motocross race at the coliseum was called the Superbowl of Motocross.

A sportswriter of the time called the event Supercross, and the name stuck. A new sport had been born, and it was about to sweep America.

Supercross Engines, Supercross Classes

Supercross machines come with different sizes and types of engines. The engine sizes and types form the basis of the three classes of Supercross. Those classes are Supercross, Supercross Lites East, for riders in the eastern part of the United States, and Supercross Lites West, for riders in the western part of the country.

Engine sizes are measured in cubic centimeters (cc). Size is one element that governs the power of a Supercross machine. Another element is engine type. Engines are either four stroke or two stroke. In a four-stroke engine, the piston in the cylinder must move four times in a cycle, from down to up, then back down and back

Supercross Lites riders race on 125cc machines, like this one.

Here riders on 250cc two-stroke and 450cc four-stroke machines race against each other in the 2006 Supercross race in San Francisco.

up, to create power for the engine. In a two-stroke engine, the piston has to move down once and up once to give about the same amount of power. Thus a two-stroke engine is more powerful than a four-stroke engine of the same size.

In the Supercross class, 250cc two-stroke machines and 450cc four-stroke machines compete against each other. Smaller machines, such as 125cc two-stroke machines and 250cc four-stroke machines, compete in the two Supercross Lites classes.

Supercross for Young Riders

Young riders have the chance to compete in Supercross by taking part in the Junior Supercross Challenge. Selected seven-year-olds and eight-year-olds ride 50cc machines in short races that take place between the regular races at Supercross events.

Supercross Machines

Supercross is a special form of motocross, and the same machines run in both types of racing. The machines have most of the same parts everyday motorcycles have, including two tires, handlebars, transmission, exhaust pipe, radiator, and throttle.

Supercross machines also differ from regular motorcycles in some ways. Their tires have knobs, or big bumps, to grip the dirt and prevent slipping. Their parts are lightweight to help them race fast, and any

Supercross machines have knobby tires and high fenders.

part not needed for racing is left off. The fork, which moves up and down to lessen the force the rider feels from jumps and bumps, is extralong to lessen the force even more. The tires bounce up and down a lot, so the fenders must be high above them.

Gas Tank

Exhaust Pipe

Fender

132

132

Fork

Gear Box

Kick Starter

Knobby Tires

This labeled photo shows some of the parts of a Supercross machine. Everything on the bike is made to help the rider move quickly on the dirt course.

Gear to Protect the Supercross Rider

Supercross is full of risks, and most riders have been hurt many times. Safety gear helps protect them from serious hurt.

A full-face helmet is one of the most important pieces of safety gear. It covers the head, jaws, chin, and mouth. Goggles protect the eyes. A special device guards the chest, shoulders, and back. A kidney belt supports the lower back while protecting the kidneys. Braces support the knees and elbows. Tall boots, gloves, and special clothing complete the gear.

Travis Pastrana was thankful for his safety gear in the 2006 Daytona Supercross.

Everything the rider wears, from the helmet and goggles to the boots and gloves, has a job to do. Riders want to be safe, so they can enjoy their sport for a long time.

The main purpose of this gear is to keep the rider safe. However, riders also want to look cool. Manufacturers help them by offering colorful gear with different styles and patterns.

The Art of the Supercross Track

Supercross takes place on a specially built track in a baseball or football stadium. Building the track requires great skill, and a special crew is hired to do it. Before work can begin, the crew must carefully measure the stadium and draw exact plans on paper. The planning stage may take weeks, but the actual building must be done quickly. Usually the track is built in less than three days, and there is a lot to do.

Here is one of the man-made hills on the Daytona Supercross track.

First the floor of the stadium must be covered with plastic or thin sheets of wood to protect it. Then thousands of cubic yards (cu m) of dirt must be brought in. Big machines, such as bulldozers, are

A Supercross track sees a lot of wear and tear over the course of the day's racing. Builders try to take this into account as they put the course together.

used to move the dirt around and shape the features of the track. A water truck is needed to keep the dirt wet so it can be packed firmly into shape.

The track's length depends on the size of the stadium, so not all tracks have the same number of features. All Supercross tracks have certain types of features, though. These include a rhythm section, a whoops section, and a step-on, step-off section. They also have triple jumps that can send riders flying 40 feet (12 m) into the air and 60 feet (18 m) forward! Locations of some famous tracks include Daytona International Speedway, in Daytona Beach, Florida, Angel Stadium, in Anaheim, California, and the MGM Grand Garden Arena, in Las Vegas, Nevada.

Tearing Down the Track

As soon as the race is over, the crew must tear down the track and move the dirt out of the stadium. They work for 24 hours straight to get the job done.

This track is being put together for the 2006 Supercross event in San Diego. The hills and turns are key features of any Supercross track.

The American Motorcyclist Association (AMA) sets the rules for Supercross events, which last all day. The high point is the evening program. There is plenty going on during the day, though. Riders must compete in qualifying races to earn a place in the evening program.

The number of riders in each qualifying race may vary, but there cannot be more than 20. The top 20 riders from the qualifying races will be in the evening

Here Martin Davalos races in the Supercross Lites class at the 2006 Daytona Supercross event.

program, along with the current top 20 riders in Supercross. The evening program begins with two

Racers at the 2006 San Francisco Supercross not only had to compete against the other riders, they also had to battle wet weather.

races, called heats, each with 20 riders. The top five riders from each heat advance to the 20-lap final race, called the main event. Riders who do not do well in the heats have a second chance to reach the main event by racing in semifinals, or semis. The top five riders from each of two semis advance to the main event. That completes the total of 20 riders who will compete to become the winner of the main event.

The Crowds Love It

There are 16 races in the AMA Supercross series, and a total of more than 750,000 fans attend the races. The races are also shown on television, allowing over 15 million viewers to enjoy them.

It's a Team Sport

Like many people you probably think of Supercross as an individual sport. That is not really true, though. There is a whole team behind the rider. Without a good team, even the most talented rider could not become a champion. All members of the team must work together well if the team is to be successful. Supercross is truly a team sport.

Tommy Hahn works with his personal trainer at the 2006 Daytona Supercross.

Machine manufacturers support a lot of the top teams. Riders who race for them are often called factory riders. Among the most famous teams are Team Makita Suzuki, Kawasaki Motocross Racing,

Mechanics work hard to make sure that their rider's bike is ready to perform at race time.

Yamaha Factory Racing, and Honda Racing.

Who is on the team besides the rider? There is a team manager, who is in charge of team operations. There is a mechanic and crew to take care of the machine and keep it in top racing condition. A personal trainer makes sure the rider

This mechanic checks to be sure that this bike will be ready to ride during the 2006 Dallas Supercross.

is in top racing condition, too. Factory engineers constantly search for ways to improve the machines.

As you might imagine, all this costs a lot of money. The money comes not only from the factory, but also from other companies and wealthy people.

Arenacross: Supercross in a Smaller Space

Usually Supercross events take place in large football or baseball stadiums. When Supercross races are held in smaller places, like ice hockey and basketball arenas, these events are called Arenacross. An arena is basically a stadium inside a building. It is smaller than an outdoor stadium, so there are not as many seats for fans and the space for the track is much smaller.

An arena is a stadium with a roof. Arenacross events are fast moving and exciting.

The smaller, shorter track means shorter races in tighter quarters. That presents extra challenges to riders. An average Arenacross race lasts less than

10 minutes. A Supercross race usually lasts more than twice as long. If you get a bad start in Supercross or make a mistake, there is time to recover and do well in the race. That is not true in Arenacross. This means riders have to race smarter.

The AMA Arenacross Series started in 1985 and has been growing in popularity ever since. This is partly due to the

> **The Women of Arenacross**
>
> Arenacross has many women riders. The first Women's Arenacross World Championship took place in 2005 at the MGM Grand Garden Center, in Las Vegas. Lindsey Jelitto was the winner.

excitement of Arenacross and partly due to the fact that it can go to more places than Supercross. Smaller cities that do not have large stadiums can still host Arenacross events. This gives more people the chance to attend Arenacross races and experience the excitement of this thrilling form of dirt bike racing. In fact, Arenacross has become so popular that a second Arenacross series began in 2005.

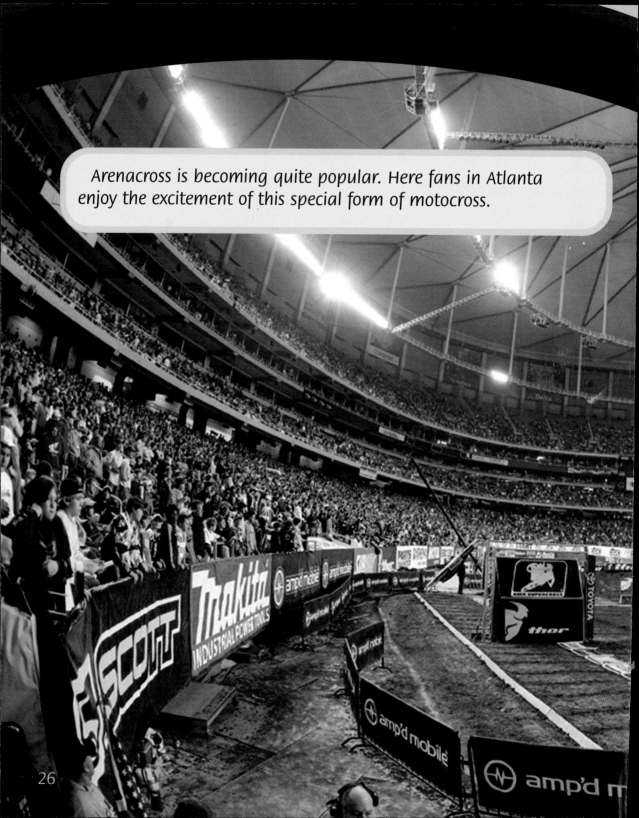

Arenacross is becoming quite popular. Here fans in Atlanta enjoy the excitement of this special form of motocross.

So You Want to Be in Supercross

Anyone interested in Supercross has many opportunities to watch races. There are also many tracks around the country where young riders can practice motocross and Supercross.

Top riders usually start racing at a very young age. Many take part in the AMA Amateur National Motocross Championships. These are held every year at country singer Loretta Lynn's Tennessee ranch. The Junior Supercross Challenge provides a way for young riders to gain experience. As they get older and their skills grow, young riders may start paying careers in Supercross Lites or Arenacross Lites before moving to Supercross or Arenacross.

In U.S. motor sports, only NASCAR is more popular than Supercross. NASCAR should watch out, though. As Supercross continues to grow in popularity, it may soon take the lead.

Supercross is a difficult, dirty, and risky sport, but Supercross riders would say there is no sport that is more fun.

What Does That Term Mean?

- **Get off**: A crash.

- **High-side**: A crash in which the rider goes over the top of the bike.

- **Hole shot**: Taking the lead in the first turn in a race.

- **Line**: The fastest path around the track or through a certain part of the track. It can vary depending on track conditions.

- **Low-side**: A crash in which the bike falls on its side.

- **Stoppie**: Riding on the front wheel only, usually as a result of braking hard.

- **Thumper**: A name for a four-stroke engine. It is based on the deep sound this kind of engine makes.

- **Wheelie**: Riding on the rear wheel only, usually when speeding up rapidly.

- **Wrench**: Mechanic.

- **Works**: Parts being tested in competition by a manufacturer.

Glossary

amateur (A-muh-tur) Someone who does something as a hobby, for free.

cubic centimeters (KYOO-bik SEN-tuh-mee-terz) Measures of volume equal to cubes that are one centimeter (.39 inches) on each side.

cylinder (SIH-len-der) The enclosed space for a piston in an engine.

exhaust pipe (ig-ZOST PYP) A tube through which the smoky air made by burning gas or other fuels escapes from the engine.

fenders (FEN-derz) Guards over the wheels of motorcycles.

mechanic (mih-KA-nik) A person who is skilled at fixing machines.

piston (PIS-tun) A sliding piece in an engine that moves up and down in the cylinder as it makes power for the engine.

radiator (RAY-dee-ay-ter) A part of the engine that has liquid used to help keep the engine cool.

rhythm section (RIH-thum SEK-shun) A closely spaced series of large bumps the same size on a racetrack.

step-on, step-off (STEP-on STEP-ahf) A group of three jumps close together made up of a low jump, followed by a high jump, and then followed by a low jump.

throttle (THRAH-tul) A handle that controls the supply of fuel to an engine.

transmission (trans-MIH-shun) A group of parts that includes the gears for changing speeds and that conveys the power from the engine to the machine's rear wheel.

whoops (HOOPS) A series of small, closely spaced bumps on a racetrack.

Index

A
AMA Amateur National Motocross Championships, 28

C
cylinder, 7

E
exhaust pipe, 10

F
fenders, 10
fork, 10

K
kidney belt, 12

P
piston, 7, 9

R
rhythm section, 16

S
stadium(s), 4, 6, 14, 16, 24–25
step-on, step-off section, 16

T
throttle, 10
transmission, 10

W
whoops section, 16

Web Sites

Due to the changing nature of Internet links, PowerKids Press has developed an online list of Web sites related to the subject of this book. This site is updated regularly. Please use this link to access the list:
www.powerkidslinks.com/motoc/supercro/